TEACHERS

by Meg Gaertner

Cody Koala

An Imprint of Pop!
popbooksonline.com

abdopublishing.com

Published by Pop!, a division of ABDO, PO Box 398166, Minneapolis, Minnesota 55439. Copyright © 2019 by POP, LLC. International copyrights reserved in all countries. No part of this book may be reproduced in any form without written permission from the publisher. Pop!™ is a trademark and logo of POP, LLC.

Printed in the United States of America, North Mankato, Minnesota

042018
092018

THIS BOOK CONTAINS RECYCLED MATERIALS

Distributed in paperback by North Star Editions, Inc.

Cover Photos: Shutterstock Images
Interior Photos: Shutterstock Images, 1, 6, 9 (bottom left), 9 (bottom right), 10, 13, 17 (bottom), 17 (top left), 17 (top right); iStockphoto, 5, 9 (top), 15, 19, 20

Editor: Charly Haley
Series Designer: Laura Mitchell

Library of Congress Control Number: 2017963078

Publisher's Cataloging-in-Publication Data

Names: Gaertner, Meg, author.
Title: Teachers / by Meg Gaertner.
Description: Minneapolis, Minnesota : Pop!, 2019. | Series: Community workers | Includes online resources and index.
Identifiers: ISBN 9781532160158 (lib.bdg.) | ISBN 9781635178104 (pbk) | ISBN 9781532161278 (ebook) |
Subjects: LCSH: Teachers--Juvenile literature. | Teachers and community--Juvenile literature. | Teachers--United States--Juvenile literature. | Occupations--Careers--Jobs--Juvenile literature. | Community life--Juvenile literature.
Classification: DDC 371.1--dc23

Hello! My name is

Cody Koala

Pop open this book and you'll find QR codes like this one, loaded with information, so you can learn even more!

Scan this code* and others like it while you read, or visit the website below to make this book pop.

popbooksonline.com/teachers

*Scanning QR codes requires a web-enabled smart device with a QR code reader app and a camera.

Table of Contents

Chapter 1
A Day in the Life. 4

Chapter 2
The Work 8

Chapter 3
Tools for Teachers. 14

Chapter 4
Helping the Community . . 18

Making Connections 22
Glossary. 23
Index 24
Online Resources 24

A Day in the Life

A teacher writes a problem on the **whiteboard**. **Students** raise their hands to answer. The teacher guides a student through answering the problem.

Watch a video here!

Some students have a hard time in school. Other students think school is easy. The teacher helps and cares for them all.

There are more than 3.5 million teachers in the United States!

Chapter 2

The Work

Teachers teach in many ways. They tell students facts. Teachers also ask questions to help students find their own answers.

Learn more here!

Teachers make sure students understand their lessons. Teachers give tests and **homework** so students can practice using what they learn.

Teachers can teach one subject or many subjects.

Teachers work with students in a big group. They also work with one student at a time. They work to make sure all students get the help they need to learn.

> Teachers often teach one **grade** of school.

Chapter 3

Tools for Teachers

Teachers use **textbooks** to teach. Textbooks have facts about different subjects. Some are about space, numbers, or reading.

Learn more here!

Others are about plants, animals, history, and more! Teachers write on the whiteboard so everyone can see. Teachers also use games, movies, and activities on the computer to teach students.

textbooks

pens

pencils

notebooks

computer

whiteboard

desks

Chapter 4

Helping the Community

Teachers care about their students. They want their students to work hard and to be excited about learning.

Complete an activity here!

It's important for students to learn at school so they can be successful in life.

Teachers welcome all students into the classroom. They want to create a safe space for people to learn. They want to make learning fun.

Making Connections

Text-to-Self

Who has been your favorite teacher? Why was he or she your favorite? Would you ever want to be a teacher?

Text-to-Text

Have you read other books about community workers? How are their jobs different from a teacher's?

Text-to-World

Why do you think it is important to have teachers?

Glossary

grade – a group of students of around the same age who work together in school.

homework – reading, writing, questions, or activities that students are given at school to complete at home.

student – someone who learns at a school.

textbook – a book used to teach a subject in school.

whiteboard – a hard, smooth board that people can write on with markers, and the writing can be erased.

Index

computers, 16, 17

homework, 11

learning, 18, 21

school, 7, 12, 20

students, 4–7, 8–12, 18–21

textbooks, 14–16, 17

tools, 14–17

Online Resources

popbooksonline.com

Thanks for reading this Cody Koala book!

Scan this code* and others like it in this book, or visit the website below to make this book pop!

popbooksonline.com/teachers

*Scanning QR codes requires a web-enabled smart device with a QR code reader app and a camera.